Mario Lemieux

THE ACHIEVERS

Mario Lemieux
Beating the Odds

Morgan E. Hughes

Lerner Publications Company ■ Minneapolis

For Bridget, Gwyneth, and Jack

Information for this book was obtained from the
following sources:
*The Hockey News, Mario by Lawrence Martin, Minneapolis
Star Tribune, New York Times, St. Paul Pioneer Press,
Sport, Sports Illustrated,* and *The Sporting News.*

This book is available in two editions:
Library binding by Lerner Publications Company
Soft cover by First Avenue Editions
241 First Avenue, Minneapolis, Minnesota 55401

International Standard Book Number: 0-8225-2884-3 (lib. bdg.)
International Standard Book Number: 0-8225-9717-9 (pbk.)

LIBRARY OF CONGRESS CATALOGING-IN-PUBLICATION DATA

Hughes, Morgan, 1957–
    Mario Lemieux : beating the odds / Morgan E. Hughes.
      p.   cm. — (The achievers)
    ISBN 0-8225-2884-3 (alk. paper)
    1. Mario Lemieux, 1965–   . 2. Hockey players — United States —
Biography — 3. Pittsburgh Penguins (Hockey Team) I. Title II. Series
GV848.L46H84 1996
796.962'092 — dc20
[B]   95–38964

Manufactured in the United States of America
1 2 3 4 5 6 – JR – 01 00 99 98 97 96

Contents

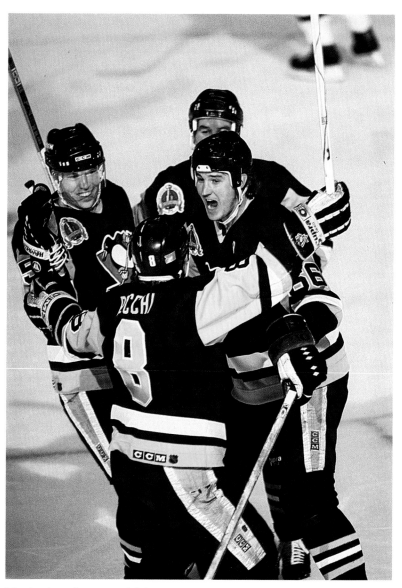

Mario Lemieux and his teammates celebrate a goal.

1
Captain Courageous

A sellout crowd shook the Met Center in Minnesota as the Pittsburgh Penguins hockey team prepared to play the most important game in its history. With a three-games-to-two lead in the 1991 National Hockey League finals, the Penguins could win their first Stanley Cup with just one more victory. Mario Lemieux, the most skilled player ever to wear a Penguins jersey, sat in front of his locker. He couldn't bend over to tie the laces on his skates because the pain in his back was so great. During the last two years, the team's equipment manager had often tied Mario's skates, the way a parent might fasten the skates of a small child. Still, Mario was ready to play the game of his life.

Across the hall in the home team's dressing room, the Minnesota North Stars knew their loyal fans would give them the home-ice advantage. That encouragement might be just the edge they needed to stop the Penguins. Or so they hoped.

Just nine seconds into the game, Neal Broten of the North Stars was sent to the penalty box for interference and Pittsburgh scored on the power play. Minnesota got a chance to get even when Pittsburgh winger Kevin Stevens went to the penalty box for holding. The North Stars' chances got even better just 34 seconds later. Defenseman Gordie Roberts was penalized for roughing, which gave the North Stars a two-man advantage.

Penguins coach Bob Johnson sent his best player, Mario, out to help kill the penalty. On the faceoff, Minnesota controlled the puck. Broten and Mike Modano organized the attack while Mario drifted gracefully into the area between them. Striking suddenly, Mario intercepted a cross-ice pass from Broten to Modano and poked the puck toward Minnesota's end of the ice. Just that quickly, Mario had created a breakaway. His long strides seemed effortless. Modano, also a dazzling skater, chased after Mario, chopping and tugging at the Penguin superstar with his stick. Suddenly, Mario crumpled to the ice in a heap. The referee called a penalty on Modano, ending Minnesota's two-man advantage.

Moments later, still down four skaters to three, Penguins defenseman Larry Murphy fired the puck out of the Pittsburgh zone. Mario, always hungry for the puck, skated past North Star forward Brian Bellows and gathered in the rubber disk at center ice.

Mario controls the puck and races away from a North Star during a 1991 Stanley Cup finals game.

Mario faked a shot and went to Minnesota goalie Jon Casey's backhand. Casey lunged to stop the puck, but Mario snapped his powerful wrists. As the

Minnesota fans gasped in horror, the puck went into the net for a shorthanded goal. Nothing can ruin an opponent's morale more quickly than a shorthanded goal.

Less than a minute later, Pittsburgh's Joey Mullen scored to make it 3-0. Pittsburgh won the game, 8-0. Nothing—not even pain—could stop Mario and his Penguins from winning the Stanley Cup.

"You dream of this," said Mario, "but it's even better in real life than it is in your dreams." Mario finished the game with a goal and three assists. "I have to be a leader on the ice," he said. "My job is to go out and score a big goal and make the big plays and lead the team. Every time you've got the chance to be in the Stanley Cup final and win it, it's the ultimate dream. It feels great. It means everything."

"People didn't realize how bad Mario's injury was," said Kevin Stevens, Mario's linemate. "*You* lay in bed for six or seven weeks and see if you can come out and play under the heat he played under."

The Professional Hockey Writers Association's voting members unanimously chose Mario to receive the Conn Smythe Trophy as the Most Valuable Player in the playoffs. Mario had finally taken the Penguins all the way to the Stanley Cup.

Pain and winning were two things with which Mario was familiar. He was going to learn even more about both in the next two years.

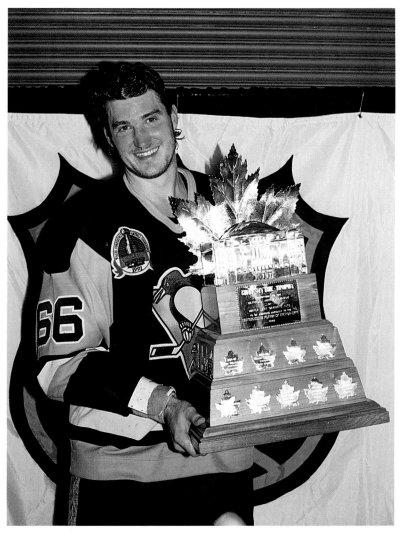

Mario scored 16 goals and assisted on 28 others during 23 playoff games in 1991. His 44 playoff points (players get one point for a goal and one point for an assist) was the second-highest total in Stanley Cup history.

Trophies and plaques decorate the walls of young Mario's room in Montreal.

12

2
A Little Larger Than Life

Mario has always been larger than life. He was born on October 5, 1965, in the French-speaking neighborhood of Ville Emard on Montreal's west end. The third of three sons, he had a fiery competitive spirit from an early age. He would battle his older brothers—Richard and Alain—in sports, board games or even footraces. Although he was slight of build and only average height, he wanted to be the best at everything he tried. He didn't win every contest with his big brothers, but he never stopped trying.

"I was always the best at the games we would play," he later claimed. "Hockey or baseball or anything physical. As far back as I can remember, I was always the best."

Mario learned to skate when he was just three years old. His mother, Pierrette, was a homemaker. His father, Jean-Guy, built houses. They encouraged their sons to play hockey. Jean-Guy was quiet and slow to praise the boys, but Pierrette was a highly vocal cheerleader. She drove Mario and his brothers to all their practices and yelled encouragement from the stands during games.

According to one story, Pierrette turned the Lemieux living room into a skating rink. She shut off the furnace and let the boys pack snow on the floor from wall to wall. With all the doors and windows wide open, the packed snow soon turned into a glistening sheet of ice. Some people don't believe this tale, but Mario insists that he learned to play hockey in his living room.

Mario was only four years old when his hockey skills caught the eye of coach Fernand Fichaud. While most children Mario's age were still struggling to stay on their skates, Mario was already stickhandling, faking goaltenders out of position, and scoring goals. He was a natural and almost immediately began playing as a center.

"At the age of six, I separated myself from the other kids thanks to the way I could handle a stick and puck," Mario said, "and never did the idea of doing anything else other than play hockey ever cross my mind. My life was one long skating rink."

By the time he was eight, Mario had a blistering slap shot. He could hit the puck over the high plexiglass behind the goal all the way from center ice! Most hockey players aren't able to hit a slap shot until they're teenagers. What made the sight even more amazing was that skinny little Mario didn't look as though he could shoot the puck 10 feet. In one game, Mario scared the opponent's goalie out of the crease simply by winding up for the big slapper. Once the goalie fled, Mario tapped the puck into the empty net. That goalie, Carl Parker, later joined the Ville Emard peewee Hurricanes and became one of Mario's few close friends.

Mario didn't have many friends as a boy. Early in his life, he seemed to decide that he liked the safety of his small family circle. He was happy to stay home and play video games, where his hand-eye coordination made him almost unbeatable.

Away from the rink, Mario was shy. On the ice, young No. 27 was a star. He was compared to previous great players such as Guy Lafleur and Wayne Gretzky. As a child, Lafleur's wrists weren't strong enough for him to fire a backhand shot. He had to work very hard to develop one. Gretzky, as a youngster, wasn't a strong skater and had to work hard to develop the gracefulness he finally achieved. Mario had no such weaknesses. He had great hands, a terrific wrist shot, wonderful instincts, and a supreme confidence in his skills. Like Gretzky, Mario's ability to see the entire rink—and to anticipate where the puck was going—helped him play at a higher level than his opponents.

Mario's skills were so advanced that he was able to overcome his greatest weakness, which was his temper. Sometimes, the players on other teams punched Mario or hit him with their sticks to try to slow him down. Mario often fought back with his stick and drew costly penalties of his own. At one point during his bantam career, the preteen center was known as one of the chippiest players in Quebec minor hockey.

In one game, Mario's coach benched him because Mario had spent most of the first period in the penalty box. His team was down 6-1 after two periods when Mario was allowed back on the ice. Mario promised to make up for his actions and he did. In the third period, Mario scored six goals to lead his team to a dramatic 7-6 victory.

In the spring of 1981, 15-year-old Mario finished his midget-level career with a league-leading 62 goals and 62 assists for 124 points in 40 games. After he turned 16, he joined the Laval Voisins of the Quebec Major Junior Hockey League (QMJHL). A "homebody," Mario was glad that he could live at home while playing for his nearby junior team.

The Quebec league was Mario's last step before the NHL. All Mario had to do was keep scoring at his regular rate and he'd be the greatest junior player ever. And his goal, after all, was to be the best.

By now, Mario needed an agent to manage his career. Quebec native Bob Perno made Mario a promise.

As a player in the Quebec Major Junior Hockey League, Mario earned $50 a week.

If he kept his mind on hockey, Perno said, he could make a lot of money someday. Mario's parents, who had always been protective of him, at first doubted Perno. But the agent convinced Mario's parents that he would get Mario a million-dollar contract in the National Hockey League if Mario kept up his scoring. They shook hands and agreed that Perno would represent Mario.

Perno became a good friend as well as an advisor. He introduced Mario to the game of golf. In the summer before his first year of junior hockey, Mario learned to play golf. He loved the game and quickly mastered it.

Perno also introduced Mario to Wayne Gretzky. Mario had idolized Gretzky, The Great One, as he was growing up, and was thrilled to spend time with the superstar. When Mario was picking a number for his Laval jersey, he wanted to honor his new friend by wearing No. 99. Perno gently reminded Mario that Gretzky was one of a kind. Why not turn the number upside down, Perno suggested, and wear No. 66? Mario loved the idea.

In 1981–82, the 16-year-old center led all the QMJHL rookies in scoring. He had 30 goals and 66 assists (96 points) in 60 games. Mario expected to be named rookie of the year. When rival winger Sylvain Turgeon (33 goals and 73 points in 57 games) was voted the top rookie, Mario was angry. "I know I'm the better player," he insisted. "I'll show them." Some people said Mario was snubbed because the owner of the Laval team was widely disliked.

During his second season, Mario scored 84 goals and 184 points. He was outplayed, however, by Detroit native Pat LaFontaine, who was playing for the Verdun junior team. LaFontaine scored 104 goals and 234 points. LaFontaine was small, fast, and explosive. Mario was big and graceful, but he often looked as if he wasn't trying very hard. LaFontaine was also friendly and easy to talk to, while Mario was quiet and difficult to reach. Mario knew there were important hockey people who didn't like his quiet ways, but he refused to change his style to suit them. Always a loner, he surrounded himself with relatives rather than teammates or friends. Still, he was stung by the criticism that he didn't try hard.

"It's not easy when you are bigger than the others," he said. "The strides are longer, each gesture appears slower, and mistakes are easier to pick out. But I have the same mind as a small player, the same heart. They say I'm overloaded with talent. But they forget sometimes that I work as much, if not more, than the others to polish my game, to be at the top of it, to get the results that everybody expects of me."

Mario spent his third year at Laval chasing Guy Lafleur's record for goals scored (130) and Pierre Larouche's record for points earned (251).

Despite Mario's record-setting performances, his Laval team didn't win the junior league championship.

He passed Larouche's mark, but on the last night of the regular season, Mario needed three goals to tie Lafleur's goal record. With his friend, Wayne Gretzky, in the stands, Mario put on a show. He scored six goals to set single-season records with 133 goals, 149 assists, and 282 points in just 70 games. He had averaged more than four points a game!

Mario had finally reached the top. After the season ended, he was voted the Quebec League's MVP as well as the Canadian Major Junior Player of the Year. As the NHL draft approached, Mario knew he had done his job. Now it was up to Bob Perno to get him that million-dollar contract he'd promised.

There was only one problem. The Pittsburgh Penguins had finished last in the NHL the previous year, so they would pick first in the draft. The Penguins wanted Mario, but they didn't want to give the untested 18-year-old a million-dollar contract. Before the draft, contract talks between the Penguins and Perno dragged on. Mario was angry and hurt by the delay. He said that he wouldn't follow the tradition of putting on the team jersey when Pittsburgh chose him with the first pick of the draft.

When the day of the draft arrived, they still hadn't agreed on a deal. Mario, true to his word, stayed in his seat when Pittsburgh team officials called his name to open the 1984 draft. "I didn't go to the Penguins' table because the negotiations are not going well," Mario told reporters later. "I'm not going to put on the sweater if they don't want me badly enough."

Mario's first National Hockey League game was against the Boston Bruins.

3
Welcome To The Show

The Penguins had steadily lost fans—and money—as they lost games, year after year. But once Mario and the Penguins agreed to a contract, just days after the 1984 draft, Pittsburgh fans began hoping for better days. The DeBartolo family, which owned the team, was counting on Mario to lead the Penguins back to the playoffs and, finally, to the Stanley Cup. His skill alone would turn the team around and put fans back in the seats, the DeBartoloes hoped.

Mario went to Pittsburgh in the fall of 1984 to see his new home and meet the family with whom he would be living. Leaving his quiet home in French-speaking Ville Emard was difficult for Mario, as was leaving his longtime girlfriend, Nathalie Asselin. A fresh-faced teenager who hadn't yet grown his first beard, Mario spoke very little English. He was already known for his shyness. Now, suddenly, he was in a big city that had high standards for its professional athletes. Terry Bradshaw, a four-time Super Bowl champion quarterback, had been booed out of town. All-star Pirates slugger Dave Parker had been physically threatened. Clearly, 19-year-old Mario faced a major challenge.

At first, Mario struggled to fit in with his new team. The seasoned veterans weren't impressed with a rookie, no matter what he had done in the junior league. To make matters worse, Mario wasn't able to do some simple off-ice exercises, such as bench-presses and long-distance jogs. But once the team got on the ice, Mario showed them his talents.

On opening night of the 1984–85 season, during his first NHL shift, Mario stole the puck from all-star defenseman Raymond Bourque. The Penguins rookie stormed the Boston zone on a breakaway. He fixed his sights on Bruins goalie Pete Peeters. Mario faked one way, then the other. He shifted the black rubber disk from his forehand to his backhand. Then Mario fired the puck over the sprawled goalie to give the Penguins a 1-0 lead just 2:59 into the game. It was Mario's first shot on goal in the NHL and it was his first goal. The Penguins lost that game, but even Mario's most skeptical teammates had to agree that the 6-foot-4, 210-pound rookie was impressive.

Bruins goalie Peeters didn't hold back his praise. "There are guys who can skate and shoot and do everything, but they don't have that hockey sense," he said.

Mario stayed in close contact with his father, Jean-Guy, and the rest of his family despite moving to Pittsburgh.

"I stood in there, forced him to make a move, and he made a move. The thing I forgot was that he's got that great reach."

Other players in the NHL soon realized that the big rookie would have to be stopped if the Penguins were to be beaten. Just as in his junior days, Mario was attacked by the league's tough guys. One time, Winnipeg defenseman Jim Kyte, who was known for his aggressive style, sucker-punched Mario. The punch left Mario with a mild concussion. Mario complained about his rough treatment. He was quoted in newspapers as saying that the Penguins should hire some players to protect him on the ice. He pointed out that the Edmonton team had obtained Dave Semenko, a fighter with limited hockey talent, mostly to protect Gretzky. He wanted the same protection Gretzky had. But Penguins general manager Eddie Johnston refused. He said, "I'll run the team. Mario can just do his job on the ice."

Hockey fans were comparing Mario to Gretzky. Fans in Pittsburgh wanted him to lead Pittsburgh to a Stanley Cup as Gretzky had done in Edmonton. "It isn't very fair to compare me to Wayne Gretzky," Mario insisted. "He's the greatest. I'll try to be the best, but it will take me more than a year to do that."

Penguins right winger Wayne Babych saw something special in the rookie center. "Mario's great with the puck," said Babych. "I've got to give him the opportunity to move with it because he's just an incredible passer."

Left winger Warren Young agreed with Babych.

Young played one full season on Mario's line and scored a career-high 40 goals. "The minute Mario gets the puck, all I have to do is find the opening and that puck's going to be there," said Young. "You couldn't ask for a better center to play with."

Halfway through his rookie season, Mario was knocked out of the lineup for seven games by his first major injury. He sprained his left knee in a collision with Washington's Darren Veitch. With No. 66 out of action, Pittsburgh's playoff hopes faded and then vanished.

Mario scored 43 goals, 57 assists, and 100 points in 73 games in his remarkable rookie season. He was only the third rookie in NHL history to reach the 100-point mark. Peter Stastny of the 1980–81 Quebec Nordiques (109 points) and Dale Hawerchuk of the 1981–82 Winnipeg Jets (103) were the first two. Mario won the Calder Trophy as the rookie of the year, beating out Montreal's outstanding defenseman Chris Chelios. Still, the Penguins finished 20th in the 21-team league with only 24 wins in 80 games.

"It's hard, you know, to start with a team that is last," Mario said. "But we have to build this team. I like to play with a team that is very low and get the team up in a few years. I think first of pride, not pressure. A lot of guys, they can't take the pressure. I think I can. I'm the kind of guy who isn't nervous, who takes life as it comes."

4
Let the Hard Times Roll

After his brilliant rookie year, hockey fans across North America knew that Mario was a star. To prove the point, Mario began the 1985–86 season with 12 goals and 29 points in his first 17 games. Yet his team still was not winning. No matter what No. 66 did on the ice, the Penguins still lost. While his friend, Gretzky, was helping the Edmonton Oilers win Stanley Cups, Mario was hearing critics say he played for his personal glory, not for his team.

Mario also moved into his own home during his second season. He set up house with his future wife, Nathalie. Mario and Nathalie had met when they were teenagers in Ville Emard.

During his second NHL season, Mario signed a five-year contract worth $3.25 million. His NHL salary was now second only to Gretzky's. Unlike Gretzky, Mario had almost no contracts with companies to endorse their products, even though his English had improved considerably. Those endorsement deals Mario did have were often threatened by his behavior. Mario often skipped videotaping sessions and public appearances. He sometimes played golf instead of fulfilling his obligations. To advertisers, Mario was an unreliable spokesman.

But Mario's work on the ice was very reliable. Just as he signed his new contract, Mario began a scoring streak that eventually spanned 28 games. During that streak, the fourth longest in NHL history, Mario scored 21 goals and 59 points. When Mario's streak ended in mid-March, the Penguins led the Rangers. But the Rangers passed the Penguins for the final playoff spot in the Patrick Division.

Although his goal of getting his team in the play-offs wasn't achieved, Mario was pleased with his second season. He finished with 48 goals and 141 points in 79 games and trailed only Gretzky (215) in total points. The NHL players voted to give Mario the Lester B. Pearson Award as the league's most valuable player. "I could have played better," Mario said modestly. "The last two weeks [of the season] I didn't play very well. I wasn't making good passes. I wasn't skating as well as I had been."

The Penguins won eight of their first nine games to start the 1986–87 season as Mario contributed 12 goals and 24 points. At one point, he had scored a goal or assisted in one in 11 straight games.

Golf is Mario's other sport. Playing with friends helps him relax. Sometimes, he chooses to play golf instead of finish deals that would make money for him.

Once again, Mario was being compared to Wayne Gretzky. By now, the comparisons had begun to divide Mario and his one-time friend. As Mario struggled to become the NHL's best player, No. 99 was his rival, pure and simple. Gretzky's agent said Mario shouldn't be compared to his client. "With all due respect," he said, "before you can start comparing Mario to Wayne, Mario has seven Hart MVP Trophies to win."

On December 20, 1986, Philadelphia's Ron Sutter blasted Mario with a hard body check. While Mario missed 13 games with a sprained right knee, his team struggled to stay in position for a playoff spot.

After the all-star break in mid-February, a bout of bronchitis sidelined Mario once again. On March 11, 1987, with the playoffs nearly out of reach, the Penguins defeated Quebec 6-3. During that game, Mario led a come-from-behind rally and scored three goals. The goals were his 49th, 50th, and 51st of the season. For the first time in his three-year career, Mario scored 50 goals in a season. Despite Mario's efforts, the Penguins finished four points out of a playoff spot.

"My goal is not to finish first in scoring," Mario said. "My goal is to win games and make the playoffs. We need to make the playoffs in Pittsburgh. I feel responsible when we're not winning and I don't have any points. It's my job out there to score goals and get assists and get the team going."

Pittsburgh fans were disappointed, and many were critical of Mario when he refused to join Team Canada for the 1987 world championship tournament. How could he turn down the chance to play for his country, people wondered. Mario ignored the criticism and offered no apologies. Instead, he played golf, and spent time alone and with friends and relatives. "I'm different from a lot of people," he told a confidante. "I'm a private person."

In the fall of 1987, Mario finally agreed to play for his country. He joined Team Canada for the annual Canada Cup tournament. During that competition, he played on a line with Gretzky. Playing with the best players in the world, Mario showed everyone what he could do with talented teammates. Mario set a record with 11 goals. He scored the championship-winning goal with 1:26 to play against the Soviets in Canada's 6-5 victory. Though he was dazzling, Mario lost the MVP race—to Gretzky.

Entering his fourth NHL season in 1987–88, Mario was dedicated to surpassing Gretzky as the game's number one star. "I've learned how to win," said Mario.

The Penguins started the 1987–88 season with a new coach, Pierre Creamer, and a new teammate, award-winning defenseman Paul Coffey from Edmonton. Mario missed just three games with injuries all season and he lived up to his nickname, Super Mario.

He set an NHL record with six points in the All-Star Game. He won a second Lester B. Pearson Award. He won the Art Ross Trophy as the league's top scorer in goals (70) and points (168). He also won the Hart Memorial Trophy as the most valuable player, ending Gretzky's run of eight straight Hart Trophies. "I though it was about time this year that I started to show my stuff," Mario said.

Although Mario was reluctant to play hockey except during the NHL season, he did play for Team Canada in 1987. The experience of playing with other great players, like Wayne Gretzky, helped him improve.

The team, however, still failed to make the playoffs. Even with Mario's brilliant season, Pittsburgh finished one point out of the playoffs and fired coach Creamer. Though the Penguins continued to struggle, Mario had clearly become a superstar.

"I'm not sure if 'dominant' is a strong enough word to describe what Mario will be this year," said Washington general manager David Poile before the 1988–89 season. The Penguins had hired a new general manager (Tony Esposito) and a new coach (Gene Ubriaco). Pittsburgh also moved second-year winger Rob Brown, who was the Canadian Major Junior Player of the Year in 1987, to Mario's right wing.

On October 15, 1988, with the season barely two weeks old, Mario scored two goals and had six assists in a record-setting game against the St. Louis Blues. After just a dozen games, Mario had 18 goals, 23 assists, and 41 points. He was on a pace to shatter Gretzky's single-season point record of 215.

The Blues had assigned Rick Meagher, an excellent skater, to "shadow" Mario. Meagher was awed by Mario's speed and mobility with the puck. "He skates so well," said Meagher. "He takes one stride and it's like full speed. He's got those nine-foot legs."

On New Year's eve, the Penguins hosted New Jersey. Mario celebrated the holiday by scoring a team-record five goals in Pittsburgh's 8-6 victory. He tied his own mark with eight points in the game, his second eight-point game of the season. During that game, Mario scored:

- at even strength,
- on the power-play,
- shorthanded,
- into an empty net,
- on a penalty shot!

Such a feat had never been done. Three weeks later, Mario scored his 50th goal of the year, in just his 44th game (Pittsburgh's 46th). Only Gretzky had scored 50 goals in fewer games. In 1981–82 Gretzky scored 50 goals in his first 39 games, and in 1983–84 he scored 50 goals in his first 42 games.

"That [scoring] is what I'm paid for," said Mario, who was still chasing Gretzky's 215-point mark. During his hot streak, Mario scored or set up 14 straight Penguins goals.

As the season wound down, the Penguins held onto first place in the Patrick Division. Then Rob Brown separated his shoulder. Mario's ace right winger had 42 goals and 98 points in 56 games before he was injured. His absence slowed Mario's scoring pace.

While Mario was chasing scoring records, his opponents were trying to clamp down on him. Opponents often checked Mario roughly. He thought some, maybe most, of the checks were illegal and protested when penalties weren't called.

New Jersey's John MacLean trips Mario. Mario says players try to hurt him because they can't keep up with him.

"I think the referees are pretty bad," he said, frustrated. "We're going to have to do something about that." The NHL's first move was to fine Mario for criticizing NHL officials in public.

Despite the harsh checking, Mario continued to shine. He joined Gretzky and Hall of Famer Bobby Orr as the only players ever to notch 100 assists in a season when he picked up three assists on February 26 in a loss at Hartford. But he lost his chances of matching or passing Gretzky's 215-point mark when a groin injury sidelined him for four games. At the end of the season, Mario had won his second straight scoring title with a league-best 85 goals and 199 points. He had either scored or assisted on 57.3 percent of Pittsburgh's goals.

Most importantly, Mario led the Penguins to the playoffs for the first time in seven years! The Penguins finished second in the Patrick Division, sixth overall in the NHL. In the first round, they faced the Rangers. Mario was held to three goals and five points in four games, but the Penguins swept their New York rivals. The Penguins played the Philadelphia Flyers in the second round. The series was tied at two games each after four games. Mario took over in Game 5. He set two NHL playoff records with five goals and eight points in a wild 10-7 shootout. Philadelphia won the next two games, however, to win the series.

Despite his 199-point season, Mario didn't win all the awards he felt he deserved. He won his second scoring title, but he lost the Hart Trophy for most valuable player to Gretzky, who had moved to Los Angeles. Mario also lost the Lester B. Pearson vote to Detroit's Steve Yzerman, who had scored a team-record 65 goals.

"I had a feeling I wasn't going to win the Hart," Mario said. "I'm disappointed but I'm not surprised. In the past, it's always gone to the best player, the top scorer. I don't know why it should change."

The Penguins didn't waste any time showing Mario their gratitude. They signed him to a contract worth $12 million for five years. He tried to persuade his parents to let him buy them a new house, but they refused. Pierrette and Jean-Guy Lemieux preferred to stay in the comfortable home in which they'd raised their family.

The 1989–90 season began in turmoil. Despite finally making the playoffs, the Penguins were divided. The players and their coach didn't get along. Midway through the season, both the coach and the general manager were replaced by former New York Rangers general manager Craig Patrick. Ubriaco later said that trying to coach Mario was like "...trying to teach a shark table manners." Mario ignored Ubriaco's insult, instead restating his goals.

"It's very important for me to get a Stanley Cup," he said, "to bring this team to a different level than it is right now. That's how I'm going to be recognized in the future, as a winner. That's something that is missing in my career."

On January 28, 1989, Mario notched a point in his 39th game to tie Gretzky for the second-longest point streak in NHL history. To his disgust, the record was set during a 7-2 loss to Buffalo. A week later, Mario's streak was up to 42 games. He began wearing a brace to help him play despite pain in his back. Throughout his career, Mario had suffered with back pain. Now, after nearly six years in the NHL, the pain was increasing from "moderate" to "severe," Mario said.

When Mario's streak was at 46 games, Dr. Charles Burke announced that Mario had a herniated disk.

Mario is a regular player in the NHL All-Star Game each winter. Here, he and teammate Ray Bourque, right, celebrate a goal in the 1990 game as opponent Wayne Gretzky skates by.

He would need surgery on it during the off-season. Mario continued to play until February 14, when back pain forced him out of the lineup. He had 44 goals and 121 points in 58 games at the time. After sitting out 21 games, Mario was still in great pain. But he made a dramatic return for the final game of the regular season. The Penguins needed a victory over Buffalo to pass the Islanders and capture the final playoff berth in the Patrick Division. Mario scored a goal and an assist, but Sabres defenseman Uwe Krupp scored one minute into sudden-death overtime to defeat the Penguins.

Mario finished the year with 45 goals and 123 points in 59 games. Although his back ached, he began a treatment plan that included aerobics, weight lifting, stretching, and back-strengthening exercises. By June, Mario was back on the golf course, playing his second favorite game. He wasn't in pain for the first time in months. By mid-July, the pain was back and Mario had surgery to repair the herniated disk. By the end of August, Mario was back on skates and eager to continue his pursuit of a Stanley Cup.

Mario can create scoring chances by making great passes.

5

That Championship Season

Will Mario's back hold up?
Will Mario ever be able to catch Gretzky?
Can Mario take the Penguins to the Stanley Cup?

The 1990–91 NHL season began with plenty of questions about Mario. No sooner had training camp begun than one was answered. Mario was sidelined with more back pain. Doctors found that he had a postoperative infection. He would be out indefinitely.

New Penguins coach Bob Johnson, an optimistic man known for his passion for hockey, knew what Mario's loss meant for the Penguins. "With Mario in the lineup, when it's 2-2 in the third period, the longer you play, the better the chance you have of winning, because you've got the best player in the game," said Johnson. "Now when it's 2-2, we've got to win by playing better hockey than the other team."

After a dozen games, the Penguins were in fifth place in the Patrick Division. Mario, meanwhile, was receiving a heavy dose of antibiotics to kill the infection in his spine. He was sidelined—unable to play and sometimes barely able to walk—for three months. "I thought this was over," Mario told a friend. "I thought this would go away and not bother me."

By mid-January, after nearly an entire year of inactivity, Mario was ready to return. He came back with a more mature view of his life as a professional athlete. "I see the game a lot differently now," he admitted. "Every time I have a chance to play the game I think I'll approach it a lot differently. It makes you think a lot and realize how lucky you are."

With the season more than half over, the Penguins were chasing the Rangers for the top spot in the Patrick Division. Mario was eager to join the run for the playoffs. "The pain is gone right now," he said. "My back is not a problem. It's just a matter of getting back in shape as quickly as possible."

On January 26, 1991, Mario resumed his familiar place at center ice for a game in Quebec. He chalked up three assists as Pittsburgh won 6-5. "I was a little nervous in the first period," he admitted afterward. "My confidence was a lot better in the second and third periods."

In his first 18 games, Mario scored 11 goals and notched 33 points. Although Mario's health was still a concern, the Penguins traded their top scorer, John Cullen, and defenseman Zarley Zalapski to Hartford.

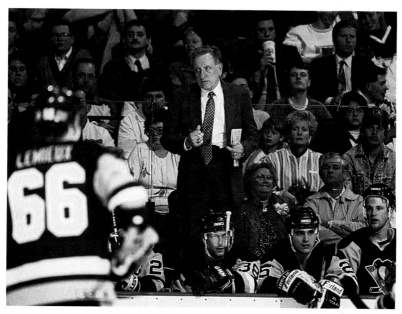

Bob Johnson, standing on a bench in the Pittsburgh players' box, was popular with the Penguins and their fans.

In return, all-star center Ron Francis, a savvy vet-
eran, and hard-hitting defenseman Ulf Samuelsson
joined the Penguins. Mario liked the deal. "There's
less pressure on me because we have a different
team than we've had in the past," he told reporters.

By season's end, Mario had 19 goals and 45 points
in 26 games, and Pittsburgh had its first regular-season division title. The Penguins faced New Jersey in
the first round. Mario's eight points helped Pittsburgh
win the seven-game series even though back spasms
knocked Mario out of the seventh game.

Ever since Mario joined the Penguins, Pittsburgh fans had expected their team to be in the Stanley Cup finals. In 1991, the Penguins were.

Playing in pain but also with great confidence, Mario scored two goals and nine points in the second round against Washington. After two playoff series, Mario led all playoff scorers with 17 points in 12 games.

Mario and the Penguins played poorly in a 6-3 loss to open the Stanley Cup semifinals against Boston. Then they lost Game 2 in overtime, 5-4. But once again, Mario took over. He scored a goal and an assist in each of the next two games, both won by Pittsburgh, to tie the series. In Game 5, Mario added a goal and three assists as the Penguins won again. Two nights later, with his team down 2-0 in the first period, Mario set up a pair of goals and then scored a goal to eliminate Boston. After 18 playoff games, Mario led all scorers with 11 goals and 32 points.

For the first time in their 23-year history, the Penguins were headed to the Stanley Cup finals. "With all the problems I was having [back in September]," Mario said, "I didn't think that I'd be in this position at the end of the year."

The Minnesota North Stars outplayed the Penguins in Game 1 to win, 5-4. Mario made no excuses for his poor showing. "I played badly," he admitted. "I had no energy. No legs." With Mario back in top form, the Penguins won Game 2 and tied the series.

But the back pain that was so much a part of Mario's daily life returned. Spasms forced him to sit out Game 3. Without their leader, the Penguins lost. Two nights later, however, No. 66 was back. His goal at 2:58 of the first period capped a three-goal burst and helped the Penguins to a 5-3 victory that tied the series. Mario opened the scoring in Game 5 with his 15th playoff goal. The Penguins' 6-4 victory brought them to within one win of the championship.

Mario could barely bend over before Game 6. Once on the ice, however, he looked invincible. On May 25, 1991, Mario led the Penguins to the most one-sided Stanley Cup-winning victory in NHL history.

"To be part of a championship team," said Mario, "especially after last year when I played most of the season with back pain, then the surgery...it's the ultimate dream." But the best—and the worst—was yet to come.

Mario's teammate, Kevin Stevens, once called Mario "the best player in the world by far."

Bad Times, Good Times

Tragedy and heartbreak are no strangers to the Pittsburgh Penguins. In 1970 Michel Briere, a can't-miss 21-year-old rookie was killed in an auto wreck. In 1983 Baz Bastien, the team's colorful general manager, was killed when he lost control of his car and crashed. In August 1991, the Penguins were still basking in the glow of their first Stanley Cup title when they learned that their popular coach, Bob Johnson, had inoperable brain cancer.

Before the season started, general manager Craig Patrick asked Scotty Bowman, the team's director of player personnel, to coach the team with Johnson. Bowman had coached teams to five Stanley Cup championships but he was stern and tough. Under the strain of playing for a new coach, the Penguins struggled for the first month. Mario, slowed by back spasms and a hip injury, got off to a slow start.

In November, Bob Johnson died. The Penguins were grieving for their coach when, at the end of November, the team was sold to entertainment mogul Howard Baldwin. Baldwin had organized a group of investors that spent $65 million to buy the NHL champions. At the time of the sale, the Penguins hardly looked like champions with a record of 10-8-4.

But Mario gradually regained his health. By early December, the Penguins began to move up in the standings. Mario trailed only left winger Kevin Stevens in scoring, with 17 goals and 37 points in 22 games. A month later, however, New Jersey's Slava Fetisov opened a nasty 10-stitch cut below Mario's left eye with an errant stick. "I actually saw the stick hit my eye," Mario said. "It hit the bone first, then my eye, right underneath the lid."

Though the injury wasn't serious, Mario and the Penguins again called for NHL bosses to do more to protect Mario and other top players. Fetisov was fined and briefly suspended. The incident scared Mario, whose chronic back pain had returned. He even talked about retiring. "It's too early to say [if I'll retire]," he said, gloomily, "but I've thought about it. If it's going to hurt me for the rest of my life [to play], it's not worth it."

The NHL still did nothing to protect Mario and other players from rough play. Mario lashed out.

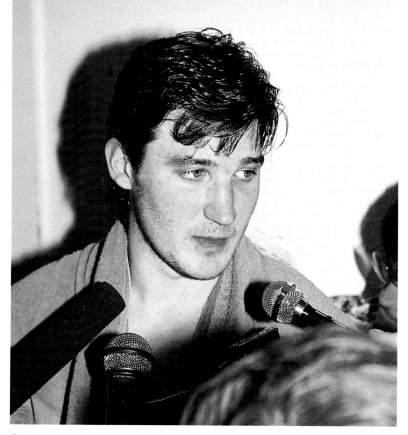

During the first eight years of his NHL career, Mario missed 123 of 640 games because of injuries. He said the league could have prevented some of those injuries by outlawing rough play.

In another interview, he called the NHL a "garage" league. (Some people have suggested he meant to say "garbage" league.) Then he said the referees didn't enforce the rules and punish players for clutching and grabbing. "It's a skating game, a passing game," he said. "I think that's what the fans want to see. I think the advantage is to the marginal player now. The good players can't do what they're supposed to do."

NHL president John Ziegler fined Mario $1,000. The NHL president reminded him that, "...despite provocation, public remarks critical of NHL officials must be penalized."

Mario was frustrated but his performance on the ice didn't show it. He had personal goals, as well as a return to the Stanley Cup playoffs, to pursue. On March 9, 1992, Mario was fourth in the league in scoring and the Penguins were fourth in the Patrick Division. A week later, Mario scored the 400th goal of his career in just his 508th game. Two days later, he was second overall in scoring, one point behind league-leading Gretzky. By the week's end, despite playing 10 fewer games than Gretzky, Mario moved into first place overall with 39 goals and 115 points in 59 games. Meanwhile, the Penguins moved into third in the Patrick Division. On March 24, Mario recorded his 1,000th point, setting up Kevin Stevens' 50th goal of the year.

Then, with only 10 days left in the regular season, the players voted to go on strike. All year, lawyers for the owners had argued with lawyers for the players about a new collective bargaining agreement. A collective bargaining agreement spells out working conditions for the players. Despite the many meetings, the two sides had not been able to agree on a deal. While the season was on hold, Mario flew to Florida to play golf. He thought the season was over.

After a last-minute deal was reached, however, the season resumed. Mario won his third scoring title with 44 goals and 131 points in just 64 games, and the Penguins finished third in the Patrick Division.

Many professional athletes say that the only thing harder than winning a championship is holding onto one. As the 1991–92 season ended, Mario and the Penguins faced that challenge. They were the defending Stanley Cup champions. Could they hold onto the title?

The Penguins won their first-round series with the Washington Capitals in seven games. Mario finished the hard-fought series with seven goals and 17 points. "We were beaten by one man," said Capitals coach Terry Murray. "Lemieux. Right now, he's the best there is."

Mario & Company next faced the New York Rangers, the NHL's top team in the regular season. Pittsburgh beat the Rangers in Game 1. In Game 2, Rangers winger Adam Graves slashed Mario's left hand. Graves was not penalized, but Mario left the game with a broken bone in his hand. The Penguins, who had complained all year about rough play, sent a videotape of the game to the NHL office. League officials suspended Graves for four games. Mario missed the next three games, but Pittsburgh eliminated the Rangers and earned a return trip to the Stanley Cup semifinals against Boston.

Mario missed the first game against the Bruins, but his teammates won in overtime. He was able to play in Game 2 and scored a pair of goals in Pittsburgh's victory. Mario added three assists in Game 3, which the Penguins won. Mario scored two more goals in Game 4 as Pittsburgh bounced Boston. No. 66 had four goals and eight points against Boston. "It's not how hard you shoot," he said later, "it's where you pick your spot." Pittsburgh had seven straight playoff victories going into the Stanley Cup finals against the Chicago Blackhawks.

The Blackhawks had reached the finals for the first time in 20 years largely because of the tough goaltending of Ed Belfour. But Chicago's defense was no match for Pittsburgh's high-powered attack.

Mario scored the game-winning goal with 13 seconds left in Game 1. He scored two more goals, including the game-winner, in Game 2. Super Mario's point streak ended in Game 3 when Kevin Stevens scored the Penguins' only goal in a 1-0 victory. "Mario takes his game up to a new level," declared defenseman Ulf Samuelsson, "and drags as many teammates as he can with him."

On June 1, 1992, Mario scored his league-leading 16th goal of the playoffs in the first period of Game 4. He assisted on Rick Tocchet's go-ahead goal in the second period. The Penguins outlasted the Blackhawks, 6-5, to retain their championship.

Chicago's Jeremy Roenick tries to stop Mario by hooking him during Game 2 of the 1992 Stanley Cup finals.

The Penguins had won 11 straight games to defend the Stanley Cup. For the second straight year, Mario led all playoff scorers in goals (16) and points (34). He accomplished this feat despite playing in only 15 games. He missed six games with injuries. He was awarded his second consecutive Conn Smythe Trophy, making him only the second NHL player to win the award in consecutive years. (Philadelphia Flyers

Hall of Fame goalie Bernie Parent won the playoff MVP award in 1974 and 1975.)

On the eve of the 1992–93 season opener, he celebrated his 27th birthday by signing a seven-year contract worth $42 million. That contract made him the highest-paid player in NHL history. Once play began, he exploded for nine points in the first three games. Mario set a team record with at least one goal in each of the team's first dozen games.

On December 31, 1992, just three months into the season, Mario scored his 100th point, giving him eight 100-point seasons in his nine-year career. He and Hall of Famer Marcel Dionne were tied for second on the all-time list of players with 100-point seasons.

"I feel a lot better than I did the last couple of years," Mario happily reported. "I feel like I can do a lot more early in the season. I'm in better shape than I've ever been. Right now, I'm at my peak. It's a lot easier to come to work when you're pain-free."

There was nothing out of the ordinary when Mario dropped out of the Penguins' lineup in early January 1993 to give his aching back a rest. The 1992–93 season was half over. His Penguins had more victories than any other team in the National Hockey League.

When he left the lineup, Mario already had 104 points—23 points more than Buffalo's Pat LaFontaine—in just 40 games. Gretzky held the NHL record for points in a single season (215). Mario had always been sure he could beat Gretzky's mark. This year, it looked as if he might do it.

While resting his sore back, Mario went to the doctor. He had first noticed a small lump in his neck months earlier. Now it had grown. Since Mario was sidelined anyway, the doctors decided to remove the growth. They tested it and found it was cancer. On January 11, 1993, Mario was told that he had Hodgkins disease. Hodgkins disease is a type of cancer that attacks the lymph nodes and causes swelling of the spleen and liver.

Mario cried when he told his fiancee, Nathalie, the results. A cousin of Mario's had died of Hodgkins disease years before. Two of Mario's uncles had died from other forms of cancer. "It's a scary thing when you hear that word—cancer," he said later. "The first day I found out about Hodgkins disease, that was a tough day for myself and my family. But the more I learned about the disease, the more I talked to my family and friends and the doctors, the better I felt. I've faced a lot of battles in my life and I've always come out on top."

In many ways, Mario was very lucky. The doctors said that because his cancer was found early, his chances for a full recovery were very good. Only days after talking about setting new records and topping his rival, Wayne Gretzky, Mario now had very different concerns.

"If I come back in six weeks or eight weeks or next year, that's not important right now," he said. "My health is more important than playing hockey. As soon as I'm ready to come back, I'll be there. Hopefully I'll be able to help us win another Stanley Cup. But first things first."

In the weeks that followed, Mario endured tiring and often painful treatments. He wore a mask to protect his face while beams of radiation were shot into his neck to destroy the abnormal cells.

"When I had that mask on, I thought, 'This is why I'm here, because of the cancer.' That's when I really thought about it," Mario told a newspaper reporter. "But as soon as I got out of there and got in my car, I let it go. I was just able to do that. It didn't really bother me that I had [Hodgkins] after a while."

By the middle of February, to the surprise of doctors, teammates, family, friends and fans, Mario was back on skates. He practiced with his team even as his therapy continued. Doctors said Mario's amazing grit was due to his athletic strength, even though Mario had never gone out of his way to stay in shape. Everyone who watched Mario could see that he wanted to get back on the ice as soon as he possibly could.

After being out of the lineup for nearly two months, Mario returned to action on March 2, 1993. He immediately picked up where he'd left off and scored his 40th goal of the year in a 5-4 loss.

Pittsburgh fans cheer Mario's return to the ice.

Despite a 24-game layoff, Mario was as sharp as ever. LaFontaine, a rival of Mario's since their junior hockey days in Quebec, had taken over the league scoring lead while Mario was gone. But Mario trailed the speedy Buffalo center by only 10 points although LaFontaine had played 22 more games. As the Penguins raced to their first regular-season title with 17 straight wins—an NHL record—Mario closed the gap between himself and LaFontaine.

Mario finished the year with 69 goals, 91 assists and 160 points, enough for his fourth scoring title. Though he played in only 60 games, he averaged 2.66 points per game. During his record-setting 215-point season, Gretzky had averaged 2.68 points per game.

Heading into the 1993 playoffs, the Penguins were heavy favorites to win their third straight Stanley Cup. When they beat the Devils four games to one in the first round, they seemed to be well on their way. They took a three-games-to-two lead against the Islanders in the division finals. Mario's back began to hurt again, his skating and mobility disappeared, and the Penguins found themselves in serious trouble. Although Mario stayed in the lineup even though his back was hurting him, the Penguins could not hold off the Islanders. During sudden-death overtime in Game 7, New York's David Volek scored with a sharp-angle shot against Pittsburgh goalie Tom Barrasso. The Penguins' season was over.

Though Mario's storybook season ended without another Stanley Cup, he showed courage off the ice that equaled his grace on the ice. When the awards were handed out, Mario took home his fourth Art Ross Trophy for scoring and his second Hart Trophy as the game's most valuable player. He also won the Masterton Trophy for dedication and perseverance. Perhaps most pleasing to him was the Lester B. Pearson Award, his third.

Through it all, Mario remained almost shy. He has continued, clearly by his choice, to be reclusive and even somewhat isolated. Despite thousands of young fans, he has always chosen the quiet company of family and friends over the glare of media attention. "Sometimes I'm not comfortable with the types of words people use to describe me," Mario said, "but I know there are kids who look up to me and that's important, too."

Throughout the 1992–93 season, Mario battled pain in his back. He battled cancer. He battled rival Wayne Gretzky for a scoring title. And Mario won on all fronts, even though the Penguins didn't win a third straight title.

As his professional life reached a high point, so did his personal life. On June 26, 1993, after many years of companionship, Mario and Nathalie Asselin were married in Montreal. Their daughter, Lauren Rachel, had arrived just weeks earlier.

Nathalie and Mario greet well-wishers after their wedding.

Mario played in just 22 games during the 1993–94 season because his back pain returned. Even without their star, the Penguins finished third overall in the NHL and first in the new Northeast Division. (The NHL reorganized and renamed its divisions before the 1993–94 season.) The Penguins lasted just six games in the playoffs before the underdog Capitals eliminated them. A weakened Mario still posted seven points in six games.

Hockey fans weren't surprised when Mario announced on August 29, 1994, that he wouldn't play in the 1994–95 season. He was tired and weak from chronic back pain and cancer treatments.

"I want to make absolutely sure that everybody understands I still love the game of hockey," he explained. "This is not a hockey decision. It's a medical decision. I feel fatigued. My stamina is not the same as it was. I think it is best to take the year off and regain my strength."

The NHL owners and players disagreed on their labor agreement again in the fall of 1994. By the time they started the 1994–95 season, there was only time for teams to play 48 games before the playoffs.

On June 20, 1995, Mario announced that he planned to return to action for the 1995–96 season. After several months of lifting weights, riding an exercise bike, and using a treadmill, Mario said he was physically renewed. His competitive spirit had also been recharged.

"This time last year, I thought my career was over," he said, "and I had no plans of coming back. But in the last six months, I started feeling stronger. I started to think I could play again. I'm not coming back to be an average player. I want to come back and be one of the top players in the world. If I can get in decent shape, I think I can get to where I was a couple of years ago."

Of course, that's when Mario—the only player in league history to win every major postseason trophy at least once—was the best hockey player in the world.

CAREER HIGHLIGHTS

NHL Statistics

Season	REGULAR SEASON				PLAYOFFS			
	Games	Goals	Assists	Points	Games	Goals	Assists	Points
1984–85	73	43	57	100	—	—	—	—
1985–86	79	48	93	141	—	—	—	—
1986–87	63	54	53	107	—	—	—	—
1987–88	77	70	98	168	—	—	—	—
1988–89	76	85	114	199	11	12	7	19
1989–90	59	45	78	123	—	—	—	—
1990–91	26	19	26	45	23	16	28	44
1991–92	64	44	87	131	15	16	18	34
1992–93	60	69	91	160	11	8	10	18
1993–94	22	17	20	37	6	4	3	7
1994–95	—	—	—	—	—	—	—	—
Totals	**599**	**494**	**717**	**1,211**	**66**	**56**	**66**	**122**

Awards

- Canadian Hockey League Player of the Year, 1983–84
- Quebec Major Junior Hockey League first team all star, 1983–84
- NHL Rookie of the Year, 1984–85
- Players' choice as Outstanding Player of the Year, 1985–86, 1987–88, 1992–93
- NHL All-Star Game Most Valuable Player, 1985, 1988, 1990
- Most Valuable Player, 1987–88, 1992–93
- Leading Scorer, 1987–88, 1988–89, 1991–92, 1992–93
- Most Valuable Player in the Playoffs, 1990–91, 1991–92
- Bill Masterton Memorial Trophy (perseverance, sportsmanship and dedication to hockey), 1992–93
- Member of Stanley Cup champion teams, 1990–91, 1991–92

ACKNOWLEDGMENTS

Photographs are reproduced with the permission of: pp. 1, 2, 6, 9, 11, 22, 28, 31, 34, 42, 45, 46, 48, 51, 59, Bruce Bennett/Bruce Bennett Studios; pp. 12, 17, 20, 25, 62, The Montreal Gazette; pp. 37, 40, UPI/Bettmann; p. 55, Reuters/Bettmann.

Cover photographs by Bruce Bennett/Bruce Bennett Studios.

Hockey puck art created by Michael Tacheny.